Here We Go Again

A Fortuna, Texas
Novella

Rochelle Bradley

Here We Go Again was originally released in *Take Two: A Collection of Second Chance Stories* published July 17, 2020 by Writers on the River to benefit Thistle Farms.

Copyright © 2021 by Rochelle Bradley
Cover Design © Christine Cover Design
Edited by Tricia Andersen

EPIC

DREAMS
PUBLISHING, LLC

Published by Epic Dreams Publishing,
LLCEpicDreamsPublishing.com

Visit: RochelleBradley.com

ISBN 978-1-947561-14-4

ACKNOWLEDGMENTS

Thank you to the wonderful women at Healing With Words who sponsored Writers on the River. They gave me the chance to contribute to the *Take Two* anthology to benefit Thistle Farms.

DEDICATION

To the women at Thistle Farms. Everyone
deserves a second chance.

A NOTE FROM ROCHELLE

Dear Reader,

Welcome to Fortuna, Texas where the men read romance. This sweet Fortuna novella can be read as a standalone but both characters are introduced earlier in the full-length novels.

You get to know Beau and Lynette in *Plumb Twisted* and meet Les in *More Than a Fantasy*. For more backstory, please read the other Fortuna stories.

Thank you and happy reading!

~Rochelle

CHAPTER ONE

Les

LES MOORE HADN'T RETURNED TO Fortuna, Texas since he'd been released from jail six years ago. He hated and loved the town. But with his brother Ben engaged, Les had decided to try to put the past behind him, at least for the weekend.

He sat on a swing at the small park that had been his refuge as a child. Ben, being older and more like a parent than his mother had ever been, got them out of the house and away from the booze and drugs as much as possible.

Les kicked his feet swinging, the balmy breeze caressing his skin. Higher. Memories of Ben saying "jump" prompted him to take flight. He landed in a pile of mulch.

A peal of laughter rang out. Les turned, witnessing a cowboy throw a boy into the air and catch him.

"Again," the little boy yelled. The man complied, and the kid giggled the whole time.

The effervescent laughter touched Les, and he smirked. The boy knocked the black cowboy hat off the man, and Les sucked in a breath. His ex's brother Cole Dart threw the boy up again.

To keep from clenching his fists, he stuffed his hands in his pockets. Les walked away from Cole and the boy toward the picnic shelter his brother had indicated.

Lyn Dart. For years, Les had forced thoughts about his first love away. She had abandoned him during his time of need. He thought their love would conquer all. No one was more surprised than him when she left town the day of his trial.

"Hey bro," Ben said, startling Les from behind. "Penny for your thoughts?"

"Hell, give me a hundred dollars and I'll show you all my texts for a year too." Chuckling, Les stood and hugged his brother. "I think you're shrinking," he said, tapping Ben's head.

Ben ran his fingers through his cropped brown hair. "No, I'm not. You're wearing heels again."

Les glanced down at his black thick-soled boots. Sure, they had a heel, but Les still had Ben by five inches. Ben had hated when Les outgrew him at thirteen.

"Where's Kelly?" Les asked, searching the parking lot.

"She stopped to get something Piper forgot. Napkins, I think," Ben said, rubbing his chin.

"Piper?" Les asked, scanning the park for Cole again.

"She's Kelly's best friend and..." Ben touched Les's arm on a lion tattoo.

Les faced his brother. Ben's forehead crinkled and his lips bowed downward. Les crossed his arms. "And...?"

Ben sighed. "And she's married to Cole Dart."

Les took a few steps back and twisted away.

Ben hurried to explain, "Cole isn't the same man he was back then. Piper has changed him."

"You mean he isn't the miserable, self-righteous, sourpuss he used to be?" Les asked with a sneer.

Ben laughed, hugging himself. "Just wait until you see him with Piper."

"I can't wait," Les mumbled, rolling his eyes. "I'm going to go walk by the baseball diamonds and try to find our carving."

"Sure, I'll get the coals started on the grill." Ben's smile faltered. "You're going to help me, right? I don't want to look like an ass in front of Kelly."

"Bro, you don't need my help there," Les laughed and sauntered away.

The baseball fields had remained as if time stood still. However, the old dirt trail meandering beyond the fields toward a small spring-fed stream was now paved.

A jogger made eye contact, then hurried past.

Les usually had that effect on people. His hulking six foot four frame, arms covered with tats, intimidated most. Smiling seemed to frighten them more. He sighed, pausing at a sign informing the public about local flora.

Sniff.

Les peered around the large sign. The little boy Cole had thrown into the air sat on the ground holding his leg, crying.

Les approached slowly, not to scare the kid. "Are you all right?"

"A thistle got me," the boy said, pointing to his ankle. The stem stuck to his sock.

Les kneeled next to the boy. He reached to pull the pricker out.

"Don't touch it! It hurts!"

"I'm Les Moore. The police officer Ben is my brother. What's your name?" Les smiled, hoping to distract the boy from the pain.

"I'm Beau Dart," he said, gazing up with red-rimmed deep blue eyes.

Les wanted to dislike the Dart boy, but the kid had spunk. He hadn't screamed for help. "I saw Cole throwing you into

3

the air. Is it fun?"

Beau wiped his nose with his arm and nodded.

"I bet I can throw you higher," Les challenged.

Beau narrowed his eyes and tilted his head, inspecting Les. "You gots a lot of tattoos."

Les smiled with an idea how to distract the kid. He extended his arm and pointed to a tattoo. "This lion reminds me to be brave."

Beau touched it. "It looks like Simba."

While Beau studied the ink, Les reached for the prickly plant and plucked it away.

"Ouch." Beau squinched his face. "You tricked me."

"I distracted you, so I could remove the thistle. How's your ankle?" Les asked.

Beau pushed his sock down, exposing a welt. "It's itchy, but it doesn't sting."

"Good. Let's get you to your feet," Les extended his hand and helped Beau up.

"Thanks, Mr. Moore." Beau fixed the sock and took a step, testing his wound.

"You're welcome. Call me Les. Before you run off, let's go see my brother, Officer Ben, and get him to put some medicine on that," Les said, thumbing back toward the picnic area.

"Okay," Beau said, taking Les by the hand and pulling him.

Once the itchiness subsided, Beau's mouth loosened, and he prattled on about his school and teacher.

As they neared the shelter, four adults turned toward Les and Beau; Ben, Kelly, Cole and a tall, friendly looking blonde who Les assumed to be Piper. The little boy took four steps for every one of Les's but that hadn't slowed him down.

When they were close, Beau yelled, "Guess what, Cole?

Les says he can throw me higher than you!"

Les slapped his hand over his face, and Beau pulled him closer. Not the best way to meet his ex's brother again. And why did Cole allow his son to call him by his first name instead of dad?

To his surprise, Cole laughed. "Probably so."

Les froze for a second, but Beau wouldn't let him stop.

"Looks like we are going to have a boy tossing competition," Ben said.

"Oh, Lordy," Kelly giggled.

"Maybe they'll add it to the rodeo," a blonde added.

"Yeehaw," Beau hollered, stopping in front of Les. He avoided colliding with the energetic youth and caught his breath.

"Don't you wish you could bottle that energy?" The blonde asked, sticking out her hand, "Hi, I'm Piper."

"Les, Ben's brother." He took her hand. "Nice to meet you. Yeah, Beau seems to have recovered just fine."

"Recover? From what?" Cole closed in with a frown. His penetrating blue eyes and dark hair, so reminiscent of Lynette, unsettled Les.

"A thistle attacked me." Beau stuck his foot out. "It wouldn't let me go. Les tricked me and got it off."

Les tousled Beau's hair. "I didn't trick you. I distracted you," he corrected. "Ben, do you have any ointment you can put on his scratch?"

Beau put his hands on his hips. "Not now. I want you to throw me, Les."

Cole bent down and examined his ankle. "It looks good," He stood and winked at Beau. "You're all clear to be thrown."

"Yay," Beau danced in a circle, then threw his arms around Les's waist. "Come on, Les. Toss me!"

CHAPTER TWO

Lynette

"HAVE A NICE NIGHT," LYNETTE called over her shoulder, waving. She hurried to her car.

Lynette had agreed to the last-minute appointment because she needed the money. When she first started at Tease Me Salon and More, the days yawned. But in Fortuna, where small town gossip spreads faster than a hooker's legs, clients had found her. The only nail technician at the salon made Lynette a novelty, and soon she had her slots booked.

Her back ached, and she stretched as she climbed out of the car at the park where she had planned to pick up Beau.

Failure after failure, college or relationships led her home where Fortuna had welcomed her as if she'd been the prodigal daughter. Reunited with her son, mother, brother Cole and his new wife fulfilled Lynette and helped to ground her. Even her recovering-alcoholic father had returned to town after abandoning his wife and children.

Fortuna offered her a new start. Beau needed a mother, not a big sister or a friend.

She squinted into the bright sunshine and inhaled the fresh

Texas air. Being in the park again brought a wave of nostalgia over her. There were fun memories of playing with kids on the playground while attending her brother's tee ball games. She'd loved hanging upside down on the monkey bars. As a little girl, she dreamed of being a gymnast. Her mother had always told, "You're petite and built like an Olympian." That dream tumbled when she had fallen out of a tree, breaking her arm.

She parked next to Ben Moore's sporty Charger. The sleek lines and tinted glass had her tempted to peek inside until Beau's laughter caught her attention. She smiled. His silly giggles brought joy to her weary soul.

Lynette spotted her brother tossing Beau into the air. She headed across the parking lot to the group of people at the shelter.

"Lyn?"

Startled by the familiar timbre, she pivoted wide-eyed. "Lee? What the f—?"

A horn blasted as a car rounded a corner, but Lynette couldn't move.

Les Moore ran toward her and lifted her into his brawny arms and out of the car's path. Her heart pounded as she clutched him. Her nose pressed against the hard wall of his chest, his spicy scent tantalizing her. Was she hallucinating? Her first and only love had rescued her. Her fingers scraped his back, wanting closer. She tipped her head up, staring into surprised silver-blue eyes. His lips quirked into a grin. Heat pooled as longing flashed.

Her heart warned: *remember the past*. Lynette shoved away from him and found her feet. She bent over, gasping.

Cole appeared at her side. "Are you okay?"

She nodded, taking his hand, needing her brother's stability and strength.

"Thanks, man," Cole said to Les.

Lynette frowned, anger simmering. Her brother shouldn't get chummy with her ex.

"Mommy," Beau called, running up to her and jumping into her arms.

Lynette forgot the men and closed her eyes, relishing in her little boy's love. "I missed you, squirt."

"I missed you too, but Cole and Piper took me to get ice cream, so it was okay." Beau wiggled out of her arms. "Guess what? I gots throwed in the air by Cole and Les. They had a comp'tetion to see how high I flew. Guess who won?"

Lynette glared at her brother, trying to ignore the heat radiating off Les's big body.

"Come on. Guess?" Beau pleaded, pulling Lynette toward the picnic tables.

"I don't know. Tell me about it," Lynette sat at the table. Piper greeted her and offered her an amber bottle. Grateful, Lynette fingered the bottleneck while Beau hopped around story telling.

"Les is strong. I think his tattoos give him superpowers. He has a lion. He told me it's for bravery."

Even the subject couldn't dampen the joy Beau's rambling caused. "How did you meet Lee?" Lynette asked. Beau crinkled his brow and tilted his head, reminding her of Lee. "Les," she corrected.

Beau pulled his sock away and showed her a bandage. "A thistle got me. I'm okay, mommy. Les helped me out."

Lynette hugged Beau again. As he squirmed in her arms, Lynette met Les's gaze and nodded. He returned the nod and moved to Ben's side at the grill. The tight fit of his T-shirt over his biceps fascinated her.

Piper sat next to Lynette, and Kelly joined on her other

side. "So, what's the deal with Mr. Muscles?" Piper asked.

"He's my ex," Lynette lamented, wanting to crawl into a hole.

"Geesh," Kelly said, leaning conspiringly close. "That was forever ago."

Lynette agreed. "Before I left Fortuna. Before Les went to jail. Before Beau."

"They were high school sweethearts," Kelly informed Piper.

The men gathered around the grill. Les stood out of the way until Ben started flipping the meat. Les motioned for his brother to step away from the grill. Ben laughed, and Cole smiled. Her brother's acceptance of her old flame chapped her.

"Why is Cole not upset about Les being here?" Lynette mumbled.

"Probably because he wants to be nice to his friend's brother," Piper suggested, rubbing her hand.

"What about his little sister?" Lynette said, crossing her arms. She squeezed her eyes shut in reaction to the whine in her tone.

Beau scurried around the table, then raced in circles near the grill. On his third pass, Les thrust the spatula toward Ben. Then Les reached a long arm out and snatched Beau as he ran by. Beau giggled as Les hoisted him into the air.

"Listen buddy," Les said, steering Beau away from the hot coals. "You can't run near the grill. If you trip, you can get burned."

Lynette's heart lurched, and she bit her lip. After all these years, could Les suspect Beau's parentage? She shivered and then plastered on a smile for her son's sake. "Hey Beau," Lynette rose and walked toward Les and Beau. "Will you show me where the thistle attacked you?" She reached for his hand and Beau clasped it.

"Sure thing, Mommy. But we gots to be careful. I don't want you to get attacked this time," Beau cautioned with a serious expression.

Lynette nodded and hid her smile behind her hand. "Can Aunt Piper and Kelly walk with us, so they know where to avoid the thistles?"

Beau formed a toothy grin. "Sure thing. Come on. Let's go." Beau grabbed Piper's hand and tugged until she stood.

"I'm up." Piper remarked, tucking blonde hair behind her ear.

"We'll be back in a few." Kelly waved to the men.

Beau led Lynette toward the baseball diamonds and took his aunt and mommy's hands. They lifted him between them when he jumped. "Again. Again!" he squealed.

Smiling, Lynette glanced over her shoulder and caught Les's gaze.

CHAPTER THREE

Les

THE VICTORIAN BED-AND-BREAKFAST'S chandelier sparkled welcome as Ben led Les through the foyer and upstairs. The grand curving stairwell had oak steps and white risers.

"Thank you for coming to our engagement party. I'm sorry we haven't had you back since," Ben said once he'd reached the landing.

Les had only been able to stomach remaining in Fortuna long enough to wish his brother well and offer condolences to his soon-to-be sister-in-law. "You've been busy with remodeling," Les remarked, glancing around the freshly painted hallway and stained and polyurethane floor.

"I know, but I wanted to see you." Ben placed his hand on Les's shoulder. "It's nice to reconnect."

"I'm glad you found a woman who tolerates you," Les chuckled.

"Me too." Ben joined in his laughter.

"So, what have you remodeled lately," Les asked, following Ben down to the end of the hallway.

"This room." Ben opened the door.

The walls appeared a blueish gray, and the molding had been painted white. Two five-foot-high windows with white lace eyelet curtains outlining the glass overlooked the backyard. On the floor was an oriental carpet in shades of reds, blues, and golds. The queen bed had a white eyelet comforter and pillows.

"We still have to work on a few bedrooms up here, but the bathroom across the hall is updated." Ben pointed to the door. "Is this okay?"

Les glanced into the backyard where an old carriage house had been made into an apartment. Inviting wicker rockers dotted the side patio. "What about the carriage house?"

"It's occupied," Ben replied, turning to leave the room.

Something about Ben's tone had him questioning his brother. "By whom?" Les asked, facing Ben.

"Lynette and Beau," Ben sighed, rubbing his chin.

"And you didn't think to tell me?" Les fumed, crossing his arms.

"With work, wedding plans, and contractors coming and going, I've had a lot to deal with. I'm sorry, but that's ancient history, right?" Ben motioned for him to follow. Les set his duffel on the bed. With a fleeting glance out the window, he left the room.

In the kitchen, Ben opened the refrigerator and removed a plastic container. "You've got to try this, bro." Ben lifted a lid, exposing green goop. "Mierda's homemade guacamole. You're going to love it."

Kelly handed Ben a bag of tortilla chips, and he opened them. "As long as she keeps making it, I'm going to keep eating it," Kelly said with a gleeful smile.

Les tasted the guac and liked it. To be contrary, he said, "Needs more cilantro."

Kelly nudged him in the ribs. "Don't ruin it for me," she laughed and dipped another chip.

"Thanks for hosting me for the weekend. I can't remember the last time I had consecutive days off," Les said. He took another chip.

Kelly moved the food to the small kitchenette table that overlooked the backyard. The uneven paver patio had new planter boxes around the edges. One box held herbs.

"Do you use the fresh herbs?" Les asked Kelly.

She blushed and shook her head. Her green eyes sparkled with mischief. "Occasionally my fiancé calls his brother for a recipe, but other than that Mierda uses them. I water them though, if that counts for anything."

"Les," Ben started. "Have you given anymore thought to the idea of returning to Fortuna?"

"I have thought about it some, but the job isn't in Fortuna, it's in Bald Knob. What's going on out there? Years ago, it was a blink-and-you-miss-it, one-horse town." Les studied his brother as Ben reached for Kelly's petite hand and squeezed.

Kelly lit up. "It's become a place where artisans have settled. There's a glass maker, a few painters, iron worker, tattoo parlor, custom motorcycle place and, of course, the gastro pub and brewery. I haven't heard you were thinking of leaving your job." She frowned at Ben.

Ben shrugged. "He just mentioned it once."

"It would be a new restaurant for the owners where I currently work. They want to expand. On my way back, I'll swing through Bald Knob."

"Maybe we could go after church on Sunday?" Kelly offered.

"Sorry, I've got to work," Ben said. "Maybe dinner?"

Ben and Kelly's planning became white noise when Les

spotted Lynette carrying groceries. Beau held a lightweight bag in each hand. Les found himself smirking, watching the kid help his mom.

He'd heard things about Lynette's mothering skills, but from what he'd witnessed, she was a helluva better mom than Ben and his had ever been. She cared for Beau. The twinkle of love in her eyes when Beau had brought her a flowering weed, and the way she'd touched his dark hair, moving it off his forehead in order to kiss him made Les happy.

"Earth to Les," Ben teased.

"Huh?" Les said, glancing at the chip he held poised. He heated and popped the chip into his mouth.

"You should talk to her," Kelly encouraged.

"No, I don't want to upset her." Les reclined against the ladder-back chair.

"You've got questions only she can answer. You are both adults now, not horny kids," Ben said.

"Horny must run in the family," Kelly teased.

Ben turned crimson but wore a lopsided grin.

"Just so you know, I'm at the end of the hall, but I wear earplugs, so I won't hear a thing if you want to get freaky." Les winked as he picked up the romance novel his brother had recommended and returned to his room.

Les studied the novel's battered cover; a bare-chested man wearing angel wings leaned over a slumbering woman. According to Ben, *The Visitation* was a Fortuna legend. The residents acted out the scenes in the bedroom and sometimes in places couples shouldn't.

"We've taken men to the station," Ben had informed.

"Stop it," Les had responded, laughing.

"I'm serious." Ben opened a closed door and pointed inside. "Is this proof enough for you?"

Les shook his head, remembering at least three colors of feathered wings on hangers.

He opened the romance and began reading. After four chapters, Les climbed off the bed and leaned against the window frame, watching the shadows cast by the occupants of the carriage house.

CHAPTER FOUR

Lynette

LYNETTE GLANCED UP FROM BUNNY Hopkins' hand and gazed out the window in time to see Les exit a silver sedan. She bit her lip, hoping he would skip the salon and leave her be.

She returned her focus to Bunny, adding a topcoat to the cherry red nails.

"You know dear, it's a shame you aren't hitched. Men are useful for some things," Bunny twittered. She continued to regale Lynette with a story about meeting her husband. Lynette cringed when the bell sounded and Les entered. Work had been her safe zone and his presence sullied it.

"Oh, heavens be praised, look at what just walked in. Mm-hmm." Bunny hummed, scanning Les from head to boots.

"That's my ex," Lynette mumbled.

"Honey, why did you let that hunk of man-meat go?" Bunny asked.

"It's complicated. We were young for starters." Dredging the past up was not an option. "How do you like this color?" Lynette directed the discussion away from the large tattooed man hovering by the reception desk.

Lynette applied the clear coat to Bunny's nails, then led her to the nail dryer. "Thank you for stopping by, Bunny. I enjoyed our conversation."

"Likewise, honey." Bunny lowered her voice, "That boy's gaze hasn't left your body since he came in. There might still be something there. Just sayin'."

Lynette returned polish to the shelf, then wiped down her station. Les approached her table and stared at a bottle of polish remover.

"Not now," Lynette uttered. "I'm working. Can't this wait?"

Les tensed, meeting her gaze, red-faced, and appearing constipated. "Another seven years?" He took a step closer.

Lynette couldn't breathe. His bulk invaded her space, hogging the air. She clamped her shaking hands in her lap.

"I need to know one thing, Lyn. Why did you abandon me? Why did you give up on us?"

She studied her knuckles, tears filling her eyes. Lynette shook her head, her raven locks curtaining her face. "Please leave," she croaked. "I can't do this."

"Why are you afraid to confront what you did?" he growled.

His words stabbed her heart. Lynette balled her fists, jumping to her feet. Her chair rolled across the room and slammed into the wall. White-hot anger fueled her wrath. "What I did? How about what you did? You're the one who ruined everything by getting arrested and going to jail."

Les's nostrils flared, and his lips curled into a snarl. The table separated his mass from her. Lynette felt the stares of the women in the salon, but she couldn't pull her gaze away from his molten silver-blue eyes.

"Where were you that night?" Les challenged through tight lips.

Words failed Lynette, becoming clogged in her throat. She shook her head again.

"Maybe that douchebag at the bar was right about you cheating on me," Les uttered, his tone bitter.

Lynette reeled, dizzy. Clutching the edge of the table, she leaned over it. "I would never." She stole a breath.

Les crossed his arms. "Then where were you?"

Lynette stared, unwavering. "How dare you barge into my work and accuse me of cheating? Get out!" She pointed toward the exit.

An evil smirk twisted Les's lips. "Did I touch a cord?"

Lynette hugged herself. Les had touched her in ways that got her blood pumping. Arguing or loving, her heart always had a workout.

With a resounding clap, Desire Hardmann hollered, "Children!" Startled, Lynette glanced at the petite, elderly woman.

Desire wore a pinched smile but continued, "This is your trigger warning. Spoiler alert: everyone has crap in their past. Whether you've got daddy issues, stubbed your toe, were passed over for a promotion. *Everyone*."

Desire pointed to wide-eyed Les. "I'd like to see you give birth to a ten-pound watermelon out of a hole the size of a quarter—without drugs. I could have been a pain in the heinie, but my situation wasn't the hospital staff's fault. Try pooping a bowling ball if you want to empathize."

Desire sighed and walked closer. "Like I said, everyone has baggage, it's called life. You can't walk through life blaming your daddy—or your momma—for not being perfect. Your past doesn't make you who you are; it's how you deal with it that does. If you can't get a handle on it, then go get professional help. Talking about it is a start, but having a shouting match in my business is going to stop. Now."

"Yes, ma'am," Les replied, shuffling his feet.

Desire smiled sincerely. "You can resume the conversation after Lynette gets off work. Isn't that right, Lynette?"

Lynette blinked. "Okay," she drawled.

"What time is that?" Les asked quietly.

Lynette's mind raced. If she could finish her last client quickly, then she'd wrap-up around three thirty. Mierda had offered to pick Beau up because her daughter, Calli, was at the same after school event at the library. Lynette didn't have an excuse not to meet Les. She sighed.

"Do you know the Tea Shack?" Lynette asked.

Les shook his head. "I haven't been to Fortuna in years, remember?"

"Do you know where the vet is?" Lynette tilted her head.

"I saw the building. It's hard to miss with the funny banner under the sign," Les said. The vet's sign requested the community spay and neuter their pets, but the town prankster had added the addendum—and weird friends and relatives. Les chuckled, defusing the tension.

Lynette rolled her shoulders. "Yes. That's the place. The Tea Shack is in the shopping center behind it." Lynette glanced around the salon. The bell sounded, and her next appointment walked in. She wiggled her fingers in greeting at the woman.

"What time would you like to meet?" Les asked, shifting his weight. The stony glint in his eyes had softened, and they glittered as if he knew a secret.

Lynette caught her breath. Did he suspect hers? "Four? It's the earliest I can get there."

"That's great," Les said. "See you then." Les bolted out the door before she could say goodbye.

Gloria the receptionist signed Lynette's client in and pointed her toward the polish wall. Desire pulled Lynette into a hug. "That young man has feelings for you. You need to say what you have to say and see where it takes you. Tell him everything, and get it all out."

Lynette clung to her boss and let the tears slide.

CHAPTER FIVE

Les

WHEN LES ENTERED THE TEA Shack, two older women in a booth twisted their necks, stopping mid conversation to inspect him. He swallowed and stepped up to the hostess stand. Mauve and hunter green tablecloths covered the tables. Botanical prints in gilded frames alternated with mirrors on the cream-colored walls.

"Just one?" a teenager asked with a smile full of braces.

"Two. She'll be here shortly." He hoped.

"I'll seat you over here facing the door, so you can see her when she arrives." She motioned for him to follow, then led him to a table.

Feeling out of place in the floral and doily-filled environment, he lowered his large frame to the spindly chair, hoping it would hold his weight.

The old ladies began talking again. They sipped tea from dainty cups with flowers.

Of all the places Lynette could pick to meet, it had to be one where he seemed out of place.

The door opened at five til four and Lynette walked in. She

met his gaze and hesitated. Rubbing her hands together, she stepped toward him. Les rose, waiting for her to sit.

"Thanks for meeting me. I'm sorry for being an ass," Les said.

"Me too. I was taken off guard at the salon," she stated.

Les glanced around. "Why this place?"

Lynette smiled. "They have the best scones."

"I feel like a bull in a china shop," he mumbled.

Lynette pushed back. "We can go to A Hole in One donut shop, if you want."

He rested his hand on hers. The warmth radiated up his arm. "No, it's fine. Now I want to try their scones." He opened the menu and scanned the items.

After they ordered, Lynette studied him. "Is it true you run a restaurant?"

Les grinned and nodded. "I'm the head chef at a high-end steakhouse. They want to open another restaurant in Bald Knob."

Lynette kept her expression neutral. "Do they want you to work there?"

Les played with the paper doily placemat. "Most likely."

"How have you been?" She leaned closer, inspecting him again. Her gaze danced over his ink, then traveled to his pierced ears. It dropped to his lips, where it lingered. He heated under her scrutiny.

"I was lost for a while, but now…" Les paused. His brother and mother flashed in his mind. "I've been working on my relationship with Ben. It's been nice to have my brother in my life again. My mother has been to see me a few times. She's sober and clean. How are you doing?"

"Lost?" Lynette pulled her water glass toward her and sipped. "That's a good word to describe how I felt, too. After the…" She stared across the room at a painting of lilies in a vase. "After our breakup, I wandered. I worked here and there and attempted school and being a mother. I wasn't good at school or motherhood."

"Not how I see it. You're a wonderful mom," Les said, leaning closer.

Tears filled her eyes, and she turned away. "Thank you," she whispered.

Their scones and tea arrived, and they sampled the fare. "I like the scones, especially the blueberry. Can you figure out the ingredients?" Lynette asked.

"Easy." He chuckled when her eyes widened.

"You're so different now," she said, tilting her head.

He sipped his tea, then finished a date scone.

"What happened that night, Lee? I know you got in a fight and beat the crap out of that dude. But why?" Lynette's deep blue gaze pleaded with him. "I never understood why you'd do that."

Les closed his eyes and inhaled a deep breath. His heart raced. Remembering the past was like picking the scab off a wound and squirting lemon juice on it. "I was wasted."

She nodded. "And so was the other guy."

Les rubbed his chin. "You were supposed to meet me, and the guy kept saying stuff about you being a cheating whore and up to no good."

Lynette gasped. "After two hours of you not showing up and that dickhead bothering me and slandering you, I popped him. I didn't mean to put him into a coma. I just meant to shut him up."

Lynette covered her face, slumping in her seat. "It's my fault, and I never knew," she breathed in a thin voice. She dabbed a corner of her eyes with a napkin. "I'm sorry, Lee."

Les took several deep breaths. While the apology seemed sincere, it hadn't answered the most pressing question. Had she cheated on him?

"Why didn't you meet me, Lyn? Were you with Trevor that night?" He'd tried to keep his voice even, but he sounded morose to his own ears.

She met his gaze. Her brows pinched together and formed a V. Her cheeks blossomed crimson. She stood, tipping the lightweight chair. "You listen to me, Leslie Moore." Hands on her hips. "I never cheated on you. You were—are the only man I have ever loved. I would never do that to you. To us."

Les's heart raced. Her words simultaneously stung and offered hope.

An awkward silence fell as the Tea Shack employees and patrons stared at them. Lynette smoothed her shirt, righted her chair, then returned to her seat. Elbow on the table, she rested her face in her hands. A sigh escaped.

"I believe you," he breathed.

Lynette peeked over her hands with tear-filled eyes. She closed her eyes and exhaled, then shifted back in her seat, lifting her shaking hands to once more dab her eyes.

Les scooted his seat next to her and took her trembling hands in his. "It's okay," he soothed.

She shook her head and tears escaped. "No, it isn't. I should have told you. I shouldn't have run away."

"Take your time, babe. I'm not going anywhere," he murmured, tucking a stray lock of ebony hair behind her ear.

Lynette nodded and stole a deep breath. She gazed up at him with red-rimmed eyes. "I was with Tish Hughes."

"Trevor's sister?" Les asked, scanning her face for insincerity.

"Before you and I started dating, Tish and I had been good

friends," Lynette explained. "When I suspected… I didn't know what to do or who to talk to. I wanted us to walk through everything together, but then what if I was mistaken. I didn't want to push you away or get your hopes up."

Les rubbed his stomach, trying to settle the butterflies. "Get my hopes up how?"

Lynette's gaze shifted to the plate of untouched scones. "I'd missed my period and wanted to take a pregnancy test."

"Pregnant? Oh shit." His thumb caressed the back of her hand.

Lynette snapped her gaze to his, and a smirk fluttered over her ruby red lips. "Tish and I went to the store and bought a test. I stewed about taking it because once I found out, there was no going back. That's why I didn't come. I swear I paced for two hours before taking the test."

Les sat on the edge of his seat. "And?" he prompted.

A wistful smile graced Lynette's lips, reminding him of the high school dreamer he'd fallen for. "I was pregnant."

Les's heart threatened to hammer out of his chest. Before the questions made it around the lump in his throat, she continued. "I freaked out, and Tish let me stay the night. We were so young." Lynette glanced into her teacup. "Then I found out you'd been arrested, and the guy was in a coma. It didn't look good."

She shook her head. "Morning sickness sucks. Smells, movement, pretty much anything set me off. Physically, I found it hard to get to the jail to visit you. Mentally, I couldn't deal with it. The love of my life, the father of my baby, could get the death penalty. And yes, I know that was the worst-case scenario. But I didn't want my baby to know his daddy died because of a stupid bar fight. I chose not to deal with it and ran away."

"I—" Les licked his lips and tried to swallow. "I'm sorry you had to go through that alone, Lyn. I wish—"

"Me too," she whispered in a mousy voice.

"Did you…?" The words caught in his throat. He squeezed his eyes shut, unable to finish the thought.

Both Lynette's tiny, warm hands held his. "Did I what?"

Les swallowed the fear. "Did you keep the baby?"

"Seriously?" Lynette rolled her eyes. "Of course, I kept the baby, you doof."

Les slumped, releasing a breath he hadn't realized he'd been holding. "Awesome."

"Beau is ours," Lynette said, tears filling her eyes once more.

"I have a son." Les recalled the sensation of tossing Beau into the air and the melodious sound of his giggles. He rubbed his face.

"I'm sorry I kept him from you." Tears streamed down Lynette's face. "I stayed away from Fortuna for a long time. When Beau was old enough for preschool, I brought him to live with my mom. I tried to get my act together, but I was lost, Lee. You had been my compass."

Les tugged her to standing, then pulled her onto his lap. Lynette started sobbing. He nuzzled her hair, embracing her small body. His joy outweighed any negativity.

"Is everything okay?" The server asked with a frown.

Les tilted his head. "Just fantastic scones."

Lynette began shaking in his arms. The silent laugh from old. She extended her arm with a thumbs up, and the server filled their waters, then left.

"I've missed you," she said, nosing his shirt.

His language skills had fled once more, and he hugged her tight, molding her to him. Les tipped her chin and brushed his lips against hers.

CHAPTER SIX

Lynette

LYNETTE SUCKED IN A DEEP breath. She waited at the Dungogh Inn's kitchenette for Beau to come home while Les searched the pantry and cabinets. His T-shirt conformed to his body, stretching as he worked. He set out a couple sticks of butter and set up the food processor on the counter.

"You're being awfully quiet, Lyn," he said, facing her over the large island.

She glanced out the sliding glass door. "I'm trying to think how to tell Beau." Her face heated. "I've enjoyed watching you work."

Les chuckled, her gaze snapped to his, and he stalked her around the island. She swallowed, unable to breathe. He stopped next to her, his belt buckle at eye height. Touching the soft denim covering his thigh, she stood. His arms slithered around her back.

His touch made her lightheaded, and she sighed against his hard chest. Les snaked his fingers into her long hair, cradling her head, tipping it back. He descended, claiming her lips with a ferocity she'd only remembered in her dreams. She fisted his shirt, wanting more. Lynette parted her lips and Les swept in. His kiss, venom to all but his touch, smell, and taste.

Her hands lifted his shirt and caressed his skin. She desired to find out if his back had the same amount of tattoos as his arms. Her hand slid around his waistband to the button fly. He moaned as she unfastened the first button, then he caught her hand, stopping her from exploring his hard body.

Lynette pulled back, inspecting him. "Listen," he hushed.

A car door, then children's squeals. Lynette broke away from Les with an apologetic glance, then moved toward the entry. The door flew open, banging against Kelly's decorative coat tree.

"Mommy," Beau shrieked as he ran toward her. He hit her, sending her backward a step. "Look what I did. It's art. Can I put it on the refrig'ator?"

Mierda and Calli entered, and Mierda closed the door. "We had fun," Calli said. "Ms. Ophelia read to us, then we painted." She lifted a unicorn painting.

Beau displayed his too, a royal blue background with a boy-shaped figure in the middle. "Is that you, Beau?" Lynette asked, steering him toward the kitchen.

"Yep. I'm in the sky," He declared, smiling. "I'm flying."

"Like a superhero?" Lynette asked.

His brow crinkled in thought. "No Mommy, I'm in the sky because Cole and Les put me there."

Lynette paused outside the kitchen and lowered her voice. "Would you like to see Les again?"

"Yep. He's fun," Beau replied, flashing her a toothy grin.

"Good. I have a surprise in the kitchen for you," Lynette said.

Beau let go of her hand and jogged into the room. "Les!" Beau ran for Les. He caught their son and then tossed him into the air.

"Here we go again," Lynette said, hiding her smile. "Beau, you're getting too big for that, and we're inside. You'll hit the ceiling," she scolded with her hands on her hips.

"Look at my pitcher. I'm flying like you make me." Beau proudly displayed his paper.

"Great job, buddy," Les set Beau on the counter. "Would you like to help me make a treat?" Les asked.

"Do I get to taste it?" Beau quirked a brow.

"How do you like those negotiation skills?" Lynette laughed.

"If that's the price I pay for a helper, then I'm okay with it." Les stuck out his hand, and Beau shook it.

Mierda and Calli joined them in the kitchen. Mierda frowned at the items on the counter. She worked for Kelly and Ben as the Inn's housekeeper and lived on-site in a suite on the other side of the kitchen.

"He's a chef," Lynette stated.

Les smiled. "Don't worry. We'll clean up."

"We are going to make a treat," Beau announced.

"What kind of treat?" Calli asked with wide brown eyes.

Beau tilted his head. "I don't know." He glanced at Les.

"Something your mom likes," Les said with a wink.

"Can I help?" Calli asked, clapping.

"Not until your homework is finished. Maybe Beau will bring you one once they are done," Mierda suggested, taking Calli's hand.

"Ah, Mama." Calli lowered her head and shuffled away.

Les handed Beau the pre-measured powder ingredients, and Beau dumped them into the bowl and stirred. "So, are you my mom's boyfriend?" Beau asked.

Lynette's jaw dropped, and she studied the interaction

between father and son.

"Where did you get that idea?" Les asked, sifting the powder into the processor. He added a softened stick of butter.

"Cole told me you and my mom love each other and dated before the tornado hit Fortuna."

Les indicated for Beau to hit the button and the machine whirred. Les met Lynette's gaze and shrugged. After the mixture had blended, he returned it to the large bowl. He let Beau dump the milk and egg mixture.

"Cole was right. Your mom and I dated," Les admitted, handing a spatula to Beau.

"I saw you hug at the park. Are you going to be mommy's boyfriend again?" Beau asked with big blue puppy-dog eyes.

"I, uh—" Les mumbled.

Beau shifted, gazing at his mom. "I like Les. Don't you?"

Lynette stood and came to Beau's side. She touched his face. "Who doesn't like Les?" She tickled Beau, and he giggled. Lynette turned her tickle fingers toward Les. "He's really ticklish. Especially here." She reached out and rubbed near his belly button.

"Hey!" he grunted, nearly dropping the bowl. He set it down, then took the spatula, shaking it at her.

"Oh no, I think I made him angry." Lynette gulped, her heart raced, recognizing the mischievous twinkle in his eyes.

"Run, Mommy. Don't let him get you."

Lynette rounded the island, and Les followed. As long as the island remained between them, she had a shot of keeping out of his reach. But the odds were stacked against her, since he had longer arms and a quicker pace. For the second time that day, Les stalked toward her. She wanted to let him catch her.

"Get her, Les," Beau called as Les rounded the island for

the second time.

Lynette stopped and pointed to Beau. "Hey, whose side are you on?"

Beau covered his mouth and giggled, kicking his feet. Les slammed into her, wrapping her in his arms so she wouldn't topple over.

Calli jumped into the room. "Is the treat done yet?"

Once again interrupted, Les let Lynette go. She stayed in his space, grinning like a fool.

"Calli, Dios mio," Mierda called. "What did I say?"

"Sorry, Mama." Calli turned and slouched away.

"We could use some help, Calli. That is, if you don't mind getting your hands dirty." Les followed her to get permission from Mierda. A minute later they returned, Calli jumping up and down.

"Lyn, can you take the kids to wash their hands while I prepare the space for them," Les asked.

"Will do," she saluted. Beau hopped down from the counter, and he and Calli raced to the half bath in the hall. Calli soaped her hands and started singing the ABC song. Beau lathered his hands and sang along. With each letter the song became louder as they tried to out sing the other. They sped back to the kitchen. Les had placed two chairs next to the island for the kids to climb onto. Wax paper dusted with flour lined the counter in front of the chairs.

"Watch me," Les instructed. He balled the dough, kneading it as he rolled. He handed a cookie cutter to each of the kids. "You start on that side, Beau. Calli start here." Les pointed to the opposite. "Press straight down."

The children worked pressing circles into the sticky dough.

"Are we making biscuits?" Calli asked.

"No. Scones." Les smiled when Lynette stood next to Beau,

examining his work.

"They look like biscuits," Lyn said.

"These are English scones," Les replied. The oven beeped. "The oven is ready whenever you guys are finished. Take your time. Perfect circles."

After arranging the scones on the baking sheet, Les used a little brush to coat them with an egg wash. He placed them in the oven and set the timer. "Now the hard part…"

"Waiting for them to bake?" Beau asked, rubbing his hands together.

"Nope. Cleaning up," Les laughed.

"Ah, man," Beau whined with a frown. He popped a dough scrap into his mouth. Calli copied Beau, and they giggled.

"That's one way to clean up," Lynette said. Laughing, she tossed a chocolate chip-sized dough ball into her mouth.

CHAPTER SEVEN

Les

LES KNOCKED ON THE CARRIAGE house door, taking a deep breath of the evening air. The inside light flicked on and rapid thumps sounded followed by "Beau don't run down the stairs."

The door swung inward, and Beau grinned up at him. "Hiya, Les. Mommy told me you're gonna read me a story."

Winded, Lynette appeared next to Beau and tousled his damp hair. "Hi, come on in," she blushed.

The small entry had another door that led to the garage, Beau's bike had been shoved into the corner, out of the way. A narrow stairwell led to the apartment over the garage.

Beau took his hand and began tugging. "Come on, Les. I want to show you my room. Do you like Legos?"

Les grinned at Lynette, then relinquished, letting Beau lead the way. Les's hand swallowed Beau's tiny one. At the top of the stairs, Beau twisted the knob on the door and entered. He let go and bounded into the room.

Les entered a small sitting area with a faded brown sofa and a pine coffee table. A small flat screen hung on the wall. On the far side of the apartment was the J shaped kitchen. Two bar stools were pushed under the tiny breakfast bar.

"Come on," Beau insisted, taking his hand again. "In here."

The hallway was the size of a Porta Potty. Each wall had a door. "That's Mommy's room," Beau said, opening the room. The bed had been made and topped with decorative pillows with words like "home" and "love." On one side, the ceiling sloped, and a dormer window had a seat.

"This is the potty. It's got fishies. I picked them out." He thumbed into the powder blue room.

Beau ran into the other bedroom. "This is my room." With hands on his hips, he took a superhero stance, fitting in with all the action figures scattered around the floor.

"Boy, your mom made a mess on your floor," Les teased.

"Not Mommy." Beau giggled and stooped to pick up Spider-Man. "He was battling a rogue truck."

"Rogue, huh?" Impressed by his son's vocabulary, Les suggested, "Why don't we pick up the battleground, so you have room to show me your Legos."

Beau tilted his head and glanced around his room. "Okay." His room's ceiling sloped as well, and he lifted the cushion of his dormer window seat. Beau dropped the toy into the storage. Les picked up a few toys and handed them to Beau to toss them in.

"Wow, look at you clean. I'm going to have to have Lee come over more often," Lynette said with a twinkle in her eyes.

"That's great!" Beau hugged Les's legs. "Why do you call him Lee? Is that his boyfriend name?"

Les chuckled at the surprise on Lynette's face. She recovered quickly. "His name is Leslie. Les or Lee are both part of his name. I've always called him Lee." She met his eyes. "You don't mind, do you?"

"It's her boyfriend name for me," Les winked. "Like my girlfriend name for your mom is Lyn."

"Ooooh," Beau drawled, and then blinked. "My Legos are in here." He pulled out a long plastic box from under his bed.

Adult conversation over. Les met Lynette's gaze, and she shook her head, chuckling.

Beau and Les sat on the floor creating and destroying for almost an hour. Every second that passed, Les fell more in love with the bright boy. His son was creative, and Les envisioned him as an engineer or working for a movie production company.

"It's time to brush your teeth," Lynette said, peering into the room.

"Ah, Mommy. We are getting to the good part," Beau pouted.

"Listen to your mom, or she might not let me keep you up past your bedtime anymore," Les said.

Beau jumped up and ran to the bathroom.

"Wow. That worked well," Les mused, blinking.

"He likes you," Lynette smiled. She leaned against the door frame, her chest out, arms crossed.

"I like him too," Les said, standing. He caressed her face. Closing her eyes, she leaned into his touch with a sigh. "Lyn." The husky tone of his voice surprised him, but after all the time apart, she still affected him.

"I'm done!" Beau cried as he ran between them and launched onto his bed. "Come on, Les." He patted the side of his bed.

Les pecked Lynette on the lips, then joined Beau. "What do you want to read?"

Beau shook his head. "Tell me a story."

Les glanced at Lynette for help, but she'd left them alone. "What kind of story?"

"Tell me about you and my mommy." Beau snuggled back into his pillow and tugged his car comforter to his chin.

"Once upon a time, like ten years ago, there was a beautiful raven-haired lady."

"Mommy?" Beau asked.

"Yes. When she laughed, it was like magic, and she cast a spell over me. I instantly fell in love with her. She had big blue eyes that saw the world with kindness. We became friends. Soon we were best friends." Les recalled a few stories of his and Lynette's tamer exploits. Beau's lids grew heavy. Even after he fell asleep, Les remained staring at the little boy. His heart could explode with love.

Lynette's shadow filled the doorway. "Les, we should talk."

Les carefully got off the bed and met her in the living room. His heart sank when he saw her pinched expression. She glanced up at him. "What now?"

"I'm hoping you'll keep me around," Les said, joining her on the sofa.

"How? You work and live far away." Lynette bit her lip.

Les scooted closer and reached for her hand, skimming his thumb over her silky skin. She laid her head on his shoulder, and they sat quietly. He pondered their future.

"My day off is Tuesday. I usually work the weekends," he murmured softly. "But I can transfer to the Bald Knob restaurant."

Lynette sighed. "You'd do that? I take Calli and Beau to the bus stop or school before heading to the salon."

"What does Mierda do? I know she can't clean that monstrous house twenty-four seven."

"She works for Jessie Barnes at Double D Intimates when she's not working at the Inn. We take turns picking up the kids. Depending on my schedule, I get the kids at the bus stop or pick them up at the library. Jessie and Desire have coordinated our schedules so the kids are taken care of. We have awesome bosses."

Lynette snuggled against him, wrapping an arm around his middle.

Her warmth reminded him of butter. It was an ingredient that added flavor. All he needed was the sugar.

Les shifted, cupping her face in his hands. She met his hungry gaze. Her tongue darted out, licking her bottom lip. Fire ignited in his heart and shot to his groin. She fisted his T-shirt, pulling him to her. Their passion threatened to consume them. He reclined her back on the sofa as she untucked his shirt and pulled it up. The pads of her fingers skimmed his abs, and he shivered.

"I've missed this." To clarify, he added, "I've missed you, Lyn. Nothing fills the hole in my heart except you."

"I've missed you too, Lee," she said, tears filling her eyes.

Les lowered his lips to hers and moaned. She tasted like heaven.

"Does this mean you're gonna be my daddy?" Beau asked, rubbing his eyes. He'd crept into the living room and stood next to the coffee table.

Les scrambled up, tugging his shirt down. Lynette chuckled and sat up. "Come here," she told Beau, patting a space on the sofa between them.

Beau shuffled over and climbed onto the sofa but didn't stop until he sat on Les's lap and leaned his head against Les's chest. Les found it hard to breathe. His heart overflowed with love. Les hugged the boy to him, feeling his steady heartbeat.

"Beau, there's something I need to tell you," Lynette said. She glanced at Les, then to Beau. "Lee is your daddy."

Beau tilted his head to look at Les. "Cool." He yawned.

Cool, indeed. Les beamed and snuggled the boy, tickling him. He squirmed in Les's arms.

"Beau, how do you feel about having a little brother or sister," Les asked.

Wide-eyed, Lynette gasped, then she chuckled, covering her mouth.

"Can I help order them online?" Beau said, then yawned again.

Les laughed and rose, carrying Beau. "Let's get you back in bed." He tucked Beau under the covers.

"Daddy, will you be here in the morning?" Beau asked, his lids at half-mast.

Les glanced at Lynette in the doorway. She nodded. Les stooped and kissed Beau's forehead. "I will."

"Okay." Beau turned onto his side. "G'night Daddy."

"Goodnight, son." Les tiptoed out of the room.

Lynette wasn't in the living room or kitchen. The bathroom door was open and the small room dark. He found her in her bedroom, turning down the bedding. She'd changed into a spaghetti strap nightgown. She straightened when she noticed him skulking in the doorway.

"Lee, close the door and lock it. There won't be another interruption tonight," she smiled, curling her finger.

Les obeyed, locking the door. Then he returned to her arms. He had everything he'd ever dreamed restored within a weekend, and he'd be damned if he let it go a second time.

The End.

44

Love a book?

Please leave a review.

Reviews are like virtual hugs
for authors.

AVAILABLE

The Fortuna, Texas Series
★Fortuna Full Length Novels★
The Double D Ranch Book
Plumb Twisted
More Than a Fantasy
Municipal Liaisons

★Fortuna Novellas★
Here We Go Again
The Playboy's Pretend Fiancée
Cole's New Song

★Fortuna Dare Society: a Book Club for Men★
Brad

★Other Books★
Dragonfly Wishes-Dragons of Ellehcor 1
Dragunzel-Dragons of Ellehcor 2
Descended-Secrets of the Fallen 1
Pandemonium in Peoria
The Secret Shelf

The Playboy's Pretend Fiancée

Welcome to Fortuna, Texas where the men read romance novels. This sweet, heartwarming romantic comedy is set in the small town of Fortuna and can be read as a standalone or as part of the Fortuna, Texas series.

When elderly Aunt Wanda announces she has cancer, Sawyer must wed in order to fulfill her dying wish and to receive his inheritance.

Stephanie accepts the playboy's proposal hoping to bring his aunt peace, but soon reality blurs and pretend feels real.

Can they keep appearances up while keeping their feelings at bay and will Wanda figure out it's a ruse?

The Playboy's Pretend Fiancée was originally included in *Beauty From Ashes: Authors & Dancers Against Cancer Anthology* published July 27, 2020

Cole's New Song
Coming May 2023

A continuation of Cole and Piper's story from *Plumb Twisted*.

An exciting day spent celebrating his best friend's engagement is what Cole had planned, but after a worrisome appointment wedding themes are the last thing on his mind.

Piper suspects something is upsetting Cole. Helping her besties create custom lingerie and decorations for the naughty nuptials kills time until she's able to sit her man down for a heart to heart. Using her skills as a lingerie beta tester might pry the words free, and his pants, too.

Can they face what the future holds together, or will Cole face the music alone?

The Secret Shelf

I'm Kate, and I work in a dream store full of local artisans' wares and indie authors' books. At the Secret Shelf rumors fly and maybe a dragon or ghost or two. Okay, not dragons.

Besides helping someone find the perfect book—yes, I have read at least one from each author, my other jobs include, but are not limited to, coaxing the statuesque new girl away from the customer service desk, dodging my boss, sipping Blissful Beans, and crushing on Brody.

Brody—what can I say beyond yum? He could have stepped out of a skinny jean ad. Hair with highlights I'd paid for, manicured hands, smells like heaven, and has a tight—well, you get the idea.

Too bad he's gay.

ABOUT THE AUTHOR

Rochelle puts an artistic spin on everything she does, but there are two things she fails at miserably:

1. Cooking (seriously, she can burn water)
2. Sewing (buttons immediately fall back off)

But she loves baking and makes a mean BTS (better than sex) cake.

When in observation mode she is quiet, however, her mouth is usually open with an encouraging glass-is-half-full pun or, quite possibly, her foot. She's a Bearcat, a Buckeye, an interior decorator, and fluent in sarcasm.

Every November Rochelle takes on the challenge of National Novel Writing Month (NaNoWriMo.org) where she endeavors to write 50,000 words in thirty days. You can often hear her cheering the Dayton area Wrimos (those who join her in this crazy pursuit).

She loves to connect with readers. You can find her on Facebook (search for Author Rochelle Bradley), Twitter, Pinterest, TikTok, Tumblr, and Instagram.

Visit Rochelle's website to sign up for her newsletter to keep up to date about future novels and book signings: RochelleBradley.com.

Made in the USA
Monee, IL
03 June 2023

34770819R20038

NR